My Son, My Brother, My Friend

My Son, My Brother, My Friend

a novel in letters

DALE C. WILLARD

CORNERSTONE PRESS CHICAGO
CHICAGO, ILLINOIS

ISBN 0-940895-17-X
Formerly ISBN 0-87784-651-0, published by InterVarsity Press.

Cover design by Janet Cameron.

98 97 96 95 5 4 3 2 1
Printed in the United States of America.

Library of Congress Cataloging-in-Publication Data

Willard, Dale C.
    My son, my brother, my friend : a novel in letters / Dale C.
Willard.
       p. cm.
    ISBN 0-940895-17-X
    1. Men—United States—Religious Life—Fiction. 2. Fathers and
sons—United States—Fiction. 3. Friendship—United States—Fiction.
4. Brothers—United States—Fiction. I. Title.
PS3573.I443M9 1994
813' .54—dc20
                                                  94-4053
                                                  CIP

For Myra

The Correspondents
Robert Cunningham
Jeff Cunningham, his son
Paul Cunningham, his brother
Philip Mabry, his friend

PHYLLIS THE PRINCESS

Well. There was this princess. Once upon a time there was this princess. Okay? Okay. Now. Her name was Phyllis. And she lived in this rotten kingdom. Well, it wasn't a kingdom exactly. It was a province. You know, a *part* of a kingdom. It was a really bad province called Warpia. Well, Phyllis's family was the ruling family there, but it shouldn't have been. Her father was the prince. Now I'm not sure that made Phyllis a princess, but that's what everybody called her. I always thought a princess was the prince's wife or sister or something. But anyway, they called Phyllis the princess.

Actually, I never saw her father. Everybody just talked about him. It was "the prince this" and "the prince that," but I never saw him. He was bad though. His name was Warp, and he was too. He was cruel and mean and selfish. I mean, I guess he was. His province was like that, so I guess that's what he was like. None of my dad's other provinces were like that.

You see, my dad was the King. He was really a good dad and a good King too. I mean, his kingdom was a great place. Everybody was happy and there were a lot of neat horses in it. And we hunted and fished and hiked and did just about everything fun there is to do. Everybody loved dad and he loved them an awful lot. I mean, it wasn't like he was a King as much as he was everybody's dad. It was great.

Warpia was the only strange thing about dad's kingdom. I mean, it seemed really weird to have this horrible place right in the middle of this neat kingdom. Well, it wasn't in the middle. In fact, it was way out near the edge. Everybody in the kingdom knew it was a strange place and wondered about it. But here's the great thing, see. Everybody knew dad was smart and wise and good, and so they were sure he had a good reason for it. Nobody ever said anything to dad about it like, "Why don't you just can old Warp and be done with it?" Now you might think it was because they were afraid to. But that wasn't it. You'd have to know my dad to know why nobody asked him things like that. Best way I can think to tell you is that they loved him and trusted him.

Well. Anyway. I have to tell you more about Phyllis. I'd known about her ever since she was born and I loved her, see. She had her bad points, but I loved her anyway. Don't ask me why because I couldn't explain it very well. But it was true. In fact, I wanted to marry her.

Now you're going to think that here's where my dad and I had our first falling out. I mean, you're going to figure that he'd say, "Why, son, with all these nice girls here in my kingdom, why would you want to go and marry some girl from Warpia?" But, like I said, you'd have to know my dad. He's not like

2

that at all. The thing is, see, he loved her too. He loved her like she was his own daughter. As a matter of fact, if you really want to get your mind blown completely open, I'll tell you something else. He told me once that Phyllis was the main reason there even *was* a place like Warpia! Now figure that one out. Well, you can't yet. You gotta know more of the story.

Now here's where it gets interesting. Because dad sent me to Warpia to rescue Phyllis. The plan was for me to win her hand, marry her, get the province back from old Warp and then live happily ever after. See, now that's not a bad story, is it? I mean, it has a nice ending and everything. Right? Well, that's what *I* thought. I figured I could tie it off and hand this thing in on time and everybody would be happy. Well, the thing went all to pieces. Here's what happened.

Dad and I decided that I should go to Warpia disguised as a pauper. You know, a poor guy. I know it's not a new idea, but it was then. You see, we didn't want Phyllis to fall in love with me just because I was rich or the real prince or anything. So, that's what I did. I got some raggedy clothes and a floppy hat and I went to Warpia.

Well, it was the pits. I didn't like it at all. Oh, they had horses and swimming holes and a lot of the same things we had in the rest of the kingdom, but the people were really weird. They looked at you funny. You know, with squinty eyes. Like they thought you were on the make or something. Like you were going to hit 'em or rip 'em off just any minute. It was spooky.

I can tell you, it made it pretty tough to find my way to the palace. I'd ask, "Can you tell me where the palace is, please?" and they'd just say something smart back like, "It's in your ear, clown," or "That's for me to know and you to find out, horse-face." You know, stuff like that over and over. One guy just grinned and held out his palm. I didn't give him anything. And he didn't tell me where the palace was either. Boy, it didn't take much of that to make me really homesick for the kingdom. And I thought, wow, what if I'd grown up here and these were the only people I'd ever known. I started to think about poor Phyllis. I really felt sorry for her. I couldn't wait to get her out of there.

Well, it took me a long time to find the palace. I never even thought about giving up though . . . at least, not till I met the old guy. It wouldn't even have occurred to me to just go back and forget about Phyllis. I couldn't leave her there to get wiped out with the rest of the Warpians. Because I was pretty sure dad was going to come down hard on Warpia some day.

I got hungry. Nobody'd give me anything. Boy, a beggar in Warpia wouldn't last out the week. I was sitting there wondering what I was going to do when this old guy came down the road with no teeth.

He acted friendly. Too friendly. Now, you're going to think I was getting just like the Warpians. You know, not trusting anybody. But that wasn't it.

He said, "Hi, kid."

4

I said, "Hi."

He said, "What's goin' on?"

I said, "Nothing."

[Miss Detwiler: I can't just go on and on saying He said, I said, He said, I said, can I? That would get pretty boring.]

"What's the matter? Can't get it together?" he asked.

"What's the matter is, I can't find the palace."

"Why do you want to find the palace?" and he looked at me squinty-eyed for the first time.

So I said,"Why do you want to know why I want to find the palace?"

He grinned and said, "Doesn't matter to me."

I said, "Good," and he sat down. He said, "You're not from around here, are you, kid? You're not from Warpia."

I looked at him a while and then I asked him what his name was. He laughed and said people called him a lot of different things. Then he got real serious and sad looking. "Why don't you go back where you came from, kid." [Miss Detwiler: I don't know if I'm supposed to put a question mark there or not. Because the way he said it it wasn't a question.] Then he stared at the ground and talked for a long, long time. He told me all about how terrible Warpia was and how there wasn't anybody or anything there worth taking back with me. Now, I wish I could remember exactly what he said because it was really some kind of speech. He cried some places and laughed some places. Sometimes it sounded like he was begging me to go back and

5

other times it was more like a warning. It was really something. I mean, for a guy with no teeth, it was really something.

It didn't influence me, though. I just stood up and walked off. I didn't like the guy. He was too creepy for me.

Down the road a ways some of dad's men brought me some food and told me where the palace was. They just stayed for a couple of minutes and hustled right back to the kingdom. I felt great after that. Seein' those men made me a little homesick for dad though. It made me want to get my job done and get back as fast as I could. That was the worst thing about Warpia—not the weird people or being hungry or the rags—it was being away from dad. Boy, that was hard. Just being in a boring place like Warpia made me remember how exciting it was to be around him. You'd have to know him to know what I mean. Anyway, it made the whole trip kind of a sad one. I didn't laugh at all in Warpia. But then I just kept thinking about Phyllis and how she'd never even *met* dad. That kept me going.

Well, the palace was something. They called it a palace. We wouldn't even keep horses in it. But it was the best they had, I guess. It was up on a hill way high above the village, and it had a big fence around it. I walked right up to the gate and said I wanted to talk to Phyllis. Maybe I should have known better. But in the kingdom you can just walk right up and do things like that. Warpia was a little different.

The guard hardly even looked at me. He was

smoking a cigarette and he just said, "Bug off," like he was real disgusted with me for something.

I said, "Look, I've got some rights here."

He said, "Is that so, Hot Shot?"

I said, "Yeah, I have."

"Like what?"

"Like I'm writin' this story for one thing."

Well, the next thing I knew I was in the jug for disturbing the peace. It was your standard dungeon. Damp, dark basement full of the ol' creepy-crawlies. I just walked out. Don't ask me how I did it. I'm writin' the story. Maybe the jailer forgot and left the door open for a split second and I walked right out.

Anyway, I went on in the palace to ask where Phyllis was. There was this maiden sitting there knitting and I asked her. She asked me why I wanted to know and I told her I wanted to talk to Phyllis. She asked what about and I told her about love that was what about.

Well, then she looked up for the first time. She looked back down and said, "I'm Phyllis."

And I said, "I know that."

She looked up again and asked me how I knew.

"I just did," I said.

"How? Tell me how you knew."

I said, "You wouldn't believe me," and she let it go at that.

"All right, let's talk," she said and went on with her knitting.

So I told her about how I'd loved her ever since she was a kid and how I wanted to marry her.

7

Well, here's where the thing started to fall apart. She laughed at me. I didn't know what to think. I always thought if you told the story you called the shots. But she laughed at me.

The only thing I knew to do was to think back and figure out why she laughed at me. So I started thinking about her.

She grew up in this terrible family. Her father (if he really was her father) was a terrible liar. I mean, he was your *orig*inal liar. Really awful. And he'd had a bad effect on her. You see, in Warpia you got rewarded for being bad. I know that sounds strange. I couldn't believe it, either. They even had a saying there: "Nice guys finish last." And that's just how it seemed to work out. Boy I hated the place!

But the more I thought about it, the more I saw dad's reason for letting there be a Warpia. You see in Warpia you could sure get a person's motives straight. If a person did good when you were rewarded for doing bad—well, you knew you had something. Now you might wonder about this. You might think the whole Warpia mess was a lot of trouble to go to just to get a certain kind of wife for me. All I can say is if you ever meet my wife (she's not Phyllis anymore; I gave her a new name) you'll probably never wonder about it again.

Well, even though she laughed at me, Phyllis said she'd go around with me some. I was different, she said. Weird was the word she used, but she meant different. You see, I didn't look squinty-eyed at her. To her, that was weird.

We'd go for long walks. Down the hill, through

the village and along the river and places like that. We talked and talked. I'd tell her about the kingdom and how different it was from Warpia. You know, how it worked by completely different rules. Well, she had a really hard time believing there could be a place like that. The first time I told her she said it sounded nice . . . but weird.

I said, "Boy if you want to talk about weird—this is the weirdest place ever!"

"You mean Warpia?"

"Yeah, Warpia. This place is terrible. It's the meanest place I ever even heard of !"

"Hm." That was all she said. "Hm." I couldn't believe it.

Well, everytime I saw her I told her more about the kingdom. She'd believe a little more each time, I think. But she'd ask really dumb questions.

Once she asked, "But how could there be a place where everybody was happy? You don't even seem very happy."

I started to explain it to her, but then I decided there was no way she could really understand the kingdom until she met dad. "Look," I said, "you'll have to meet the King before you can understand all this."

She looked at me like that wasn't a very good explanation. So I said, "Trust me. Okay? Can't you just believe what I'm telling you because you trust me?" She still didn't look too sure.

"Look, Phyllis," I said, "I'm not going to make you go with me. If you don't trust me we're not going to get anywhere."

9

It was quite a while before I felt it was safe to tell her who I was. Well, you could've knocked her over with a piece of lint.

"You're the King's boy?"

"That's right," I said.

"Really?"

"Really."

"Boy, you better not *tell* anybody about that."

"Why?" I asked.

"Well, you'd just better not, that's all."

Then I really floored her. I leaned over and whispered in her ear, "I'm the one who's writing this story." Well, she flat flipped her lid. She flat flipped her lid.

I think she'd have gone with me that night, but right then some of old Warp's guards jumped out of the bushes and grabbed me.

Well, Phyllis is really pretty. She's a lot of fun, and she has blonde hair and a nice smile and a good personality. But she lied through her teeth at the trial.

She said, "*I* don't know who he is. I met him down in the village and he sweet talked me and I just thought he was a nice guy."

Well, I don't hold it against her. She was scared, and she grew up in this rotten family in this terrible province. I still love her. I'm going to change her so she won't lie like that in the next chapter.

They decided to hang me. I told you it was a terrible place. They said old Warp was the real prince and I was a phony. Then the guard at the gate told them what I'd said about how I was writing this story and they said boy that took the cake.

So they did hang me. Tried to kick me right out of my own story. They've got a pretty big surprise coming.

Phyllis cried a lot because she really did love me. She just couldn't help herself in what she did. Like I said, I'm going to make her different in the next chapter. That is, if she'll go along with it.

[Miss Detwiler: I'm sorry I didn't get this finished. I have a math test fourth period and I also had trouble with the story, as you can see. But, I've never done this "first person" thing before. Did I do it right? Anyway, I had no idea it was going to need to be this long. It's going to take at least one more chapter and maybe two. I'll try to hand the rest in Monday. Okay? I'm sorry.]

Dear Dad,

I hope you'll enjoy "Phyllis the Princess." It was passed along to me by one of the sophomore English teachers. (I think you'll agree that her young author knows more than he knows!) It's a custom among the English teachers to show one another anything that keeps our humor up. We need all our mutual encouragement to keep ourselves reading these things and correcting the same errors over and over. But there's no way around it. It's at once the worst drudgery and the most useful thing we do.

But here now. You ask for more about this Laura who keeps "popping up" in my letters, and I am wary. Don't think you'll lure me into some orgy of hollow-eyed sentimental excess. Oh, the material is there. She has it all—eyes, smile, brittleness, soft-ness—enough to keep a few poets in work for weeks. (Think of a WPA project for unemployed poets: "Alright now, give us six rhyming couplets on this girl here. When you're through with that we'll have something else thought up. You may all check out nibs, paper, ink, etc. at central supply. Report back here in three weeks.")

She's brilliant. It's not her intelligence alone. I mean, she's a bright burner—the flame from her wick is higher, denser. And any fuel will do. That's what unsettles me. She's widely read, though not well-educated in any true sense. She can't, or doesn't, distinguish. She absorbs. I'd have her absorb a bit more from healthier sources. And she's beginning to.

Good grief! I've just read over the last paragraph. Don't worry. I'm no moth! I have not a fatalistic bone in my body. She is a bit irresistible to the plodding likes of me, I admit. But see, no one plods into a candle flame. I'm in no danger unless I learn to fly. Still, no harm, I suppose, in watching for any small suspicious lumps that might begin to punch out the back of my shirt.

No, she's not a teacher. She's a close friend of one of the art instructors here. Laura is a would-be artist herself—a pretty good one, actually, though she doesn't make a living at it. (She doesn't have to. Same old story: her father is wealthy—a cold cream magnate or something—and indulgent. So she . . . dabbles.)

She runs with a pretty artsy crowd and wants me in it. I don't like her friends much, but she does fascinate me. And what a puzzle she is: brought up on food I've only read about in books; thinking thoughts I've never thought; taking my giants for pygmies and fearing as dragons what I think are lizards. She moons over Sylvia Plath's verse and mourns the woman's death as of a goddess.

I am far more the alien than she is in this city. Laura passes for a sage here. They hold her in awe. But I know (and so does she) that she is only smart. Alas, she is that. She is to the corner and back while I am getting in position for the race, thinking rings and spirals around me. Yet when I speak she listens. And I am more than a curiosity to her for I speak of things she has rarely even dreamed. Most of her dreams are bad. I long to see peace in her. What should such a dance as hers look like if done in peace! I want to see it.

Your son,
Jeff

Dear Paul,

We have greatly appreciated the short notes from Edith. They have, at least, assured us that you are alive. Maggie thinks she reads things between Edith's lines. I assure her that what she reads in is outlandish—that, after all, my knowledge of my own brother counts for a bit more than her facitious theories. Nevertheless, I cannot put off forever her bald insistence that "*something* must be going on with Paul."

Frankly, the absence of your weekly letter in my hand has left something of a hole in my little routines. Mags used to say there was no living with me till Monday if your note somehow missed the week's mail. I'm afraid she was right. So you can imagine what I've put her through the last few weeks. For her sake, then . . .

I shouldn't pry, I suppose, but could your letterly silence be at all connected with the dream you mentioned in your last? If it is, then Maggie shall win most of her points and I shall retire from the field in momentary disgrace. Not that I'd have you hide the truth for the sake of my victory, for all that. She is a formidable opponent, but I win my share. I should only have to take her to dinner or some such thing, and we could both use the occasion well.

She's a gracious winner.

Mabry was here Sunday and he remains in top form. He was on his way to the coast to do a bit of research for an article he's working on (a muckraker, I'll warrant, but of course he wouldn't tell us). By the way, he swore, and with a straight face, that you and he and I never robbed Huddleston's pear orchard. But I'm positive it was Mabry who was with us when the old man lay in wait with birdshot. Can you help me out here? Of course Mabry is famous (at least with you and me) for this kind of put-on. So the next time I see him he'll probably deny he ever denied it! And I'll partly believe him. I don't know how he does it.

Jeff is getting a little tired of high-school teaching, I think. I try to encourage him every time I have the chance. I believe he is convinced, now, that man (or at least, boy) is naturally resistant to learning. He speaks of certain "antibodies" that seem to leap to the defense whenever and wherever ignorance is seriously threatened. He wonders if the university is any different, and I tell him that it is but only in certain technical respects. For example, the antibodies there are more mature—that is, more subtle, more deadly. Do you agree?

Paul, I find myself returning over and over to one thought. It is a fear. I have tried to write around it, but we are too close for that. Have I offended? Our last few exchanges were heated. I can't well remember what I may have said in all of them. But, please, you know—don't you?—that I would never try to wound you. I confess that I enjoyed the argu-

17

ment. But then I thought you did too. I know—and it is the greatest pain in my life (I do not exaggerate) to know that we are at complete odds on the subject of this controversy. Still, you are the brother I love, the companion of my youth. I would give up my life (and with a light heart, too) if you could come with me on this, but never would I dream of trying to bully you in the matter. Not that I could. You are the man whose mind I respect above all others. You know that. It is why I enjoy the game so much.

I don't mean to say it's only a game with me. But our ability to treat it at that level, at least, has given us a chance to be together in it even if in a strange sense. That, for me, is so much better than nothing.

Please tell me—tell me specifically—if there is some complaint. You'll not find a readier penitent.

Your brother,
Robert

Dear Robert,

You asked me to be specific about my complaints.
As you wish.

They say he sits as a refiner, a purifier of silver.
And that he will put the fire to you until you—what?
Yield the metal?

Well, who can take that kind of insinuation? Is the
whole business designed to get one's hackles up?
What am I? Dross? I am what I am. I have weak-
nesses. I have strengths. And certain attributes . . .
are not totally unsubstantial. I do not wish to be
immodest, but must I close my eyes and say I have
no love in me, that I have never done a kind thing?
Some things in myself I would certainly eschew.
Others . . . I'll stand behind.

Who could bear it: to see all one's achievements
flare away, a brief, orange interruption in some
steady blue flame? Who could say there'd be any
metal there—I mean, by his standards? Have I no
case at all? Yes, and here! They say I was made by
him, and even worse, for him. Am I a toy? An enter-
tainment?

Do you see it? I can't speak for you, of course, but I
have stronger ambitions for myself, for my own *self*,
than that. Somehow I fancy myself of some importance (small, perhaps to him; less than nothing, per-

haps; but to me, some importance).

Oh, it goes on and on, Robert. I am clay to his potter. And the clay has no right to talk back, they say. Ah, but why this voice? Why do I find myself capable of thought, of volition? Do you follow my gist?

Well, that's it, I think. Let me hear from you.

With affection,
Paul

P.S. It was most assuredly Mabry. Don't let him gull you like that. You were always a pushover for him. Now that you've dug them up, I remember what great times those were! I think it was great good fortune for Father to have been stationed in England all those years. Can you imagine the poverty of a childhood without Philip Mabry? I miss you both: the jolly liar and the little wide-eyed naif. Curse this distance between us.

P.

Dear Jeff,

I have been to the library. I dug out and read every work of Sylvia Plath's I could find. I lay her poems down with moisture in the eye and a sting of sulphur on the lips.

I call her brilliant, like your Laura, and long to see her at peace. For what would a gift such as hers be like, spoken in peace? Oh, they will argue with me here, I well know. And perhaps they are right. Perhaps the gift goes out with the angst. Then *let* it go.

Love,
Dad

Dear Paul,

I'm sure it was cold and grey after your letter came, as well as before. It only seemed to turn warm. You see what you can do for this household with just a few minutes and pen and ink?

Just wait till I see Mabry again! He'll have a pretty time working his way out of two on one. It was always his complaint, remember? Blood thicker than water. Secretly, he enjoyed it, gloating that it took two of us to beat him.

Exams are on me and, no doubt, on you. Maggie pads in and out on cat feet, bringing coffee, meals, etc. How does Edith handle the tribulation? I've never seen her out of sorts. Does her equanimity have no limits?

I have a rather dull crop this semester. They are polite, punctual, and dull. Their eyes begin to glaze over about twenty minutes into the hour and I am sure my career is finished. Then one of them comes up to tell me I'm the most interesting professor she has ever had, and I begin to worry about her career instead of mine. There does seem to be a deterioration going on in the arts here, but I balk at thinking of it. An old woman (in her eighties) once complained to Maggie that everybody in the world seemed to be dying off. Perhaps my feeling about the downhill slide of the college is a similar projection.

Where is your book now? At the publisher's, I hope? I let a colleague here read the Hemingway chapter (I hope you don't mind), and he and I are in enthusiastic agreement. The thesis, he feels, is remarkably well laid out and does some much needed shredding of a few specious theories about the war business. I can't wait to see the whole in print. For myself, I selfishly look forward to a certain celebrity by association. But, most of all, I long for a return to health in criticism, and I dream that your book may well bring it about almost single-handedly. If I gush, forgive me; you know I do not flatter. I am just so excited about this particular work.

If you should happen to receive a rejection slip or two, do not waiver; no dallying over revisions. Just shake the dust off your feet and pack the thing off to another publisher. It's ready, Paul, the way it is.

Well. Exams are exams.

With love,
Robert

Dad,

Yech! I do not understand this modern love affair with death! These poets reek with it. Laura is tantalized by their dark river Styx. Her heroes and heroines wade out and sometimes disappear. She sits on the bank, transfixed, imagining that, yes, after all, evil is good and death is life. Damnation! Will they forever prefer darkness to light?

It is all Warp's work. He is behind the thinnest film of gauze in this place. I am one with James and John: Boanerges, the three of us! Let the fire fall and, if I turn back to look, let me turn to salt!

I want to bring Laura home. Sometimes I think if she could only be around you and Mother for a while she would start to dream good dreams. Dad, there are whole populations in this end of the country who do not know anything of peace and joy. In fact their artists, their jesters, tell them that these are cheap thrills and that beneath them are the deep things—the misery, the anguish which drowns all. They love it here. They take it whole and ask their analysts why they want to die.

Hope is the butt of the universally known joke in their company. No one quite remembers what the joke was, but that doesn't matter. The trick is to laugh knowingly at anything hopeful. They are squinty-eyed Warpians, the lot of them. I would take her out of this if only for a weekend.

Jeff

Dear Jeff,

Your calling down of the fire I understand. You and I, I think, are in very little danger of turning to salt. Our disobedience would be the opposite. While God says, "I spread out my hands all the day to a rebellious people . . . " we're ready to lower ours a bit too early in the afternoon. Must we not keep our hands wide while it is yet day? Soon enough the night when that awesome Back will turn. Dare we turn ours a moment sooner?

You are, of course, welcome to bring Laura for a visit. When will you come?

Dad

Dear Robert,

Well, I'm heady with your praise this A.M. The book is at the publisher's, though I haven't heard a word since sending it in nine weeks ago today. It is rather like awaiting a jury. If they keep the case overnight, is that good?

It has been your encouragement since the beginning, of course, that kept the book going. Your prefortifications against a rejection slip or two are welcome. I can't predict how many I would be able to endure without a loss of nerve.

As to Jeff and his "antibodies" (antiminds?) I heartily agree with you both. The most pernicious of all, I find to be something I should describe as the "what-good-is-it?" variant. I have a hotbed of the most virile laboratory specimens of this variety teeming about in my survey class. I have never yet answered that question for students. Who indeed could—at least for this generation? The closest I've ever come to trying was last term when I said that once the question is asked the answer is already impossible. Does that make any sense to you? It made perfect sense to me at the time. In fact, I thought it a brilliant stroke. The students found it utterly lackluster.

Oh. I should tell you that I think I've hit upon (or sat upon) some incontrovertible evidence for you to use on Mabry regarding the orchard incident. I am sure that I have (and I'll wager he has something similar) rather "hard" evidence still resident in the posterior area of my body. I don't know the state of the art of matching up bits of birdshot, but if there is any precise method available I am certain his birdshot and mine could be traced to a single shell fired from old Huddleston's gun. Where were you when the shot went off, by the way? I don't remember you picking anything out of your pants!

But come now, Robert. You answered not a single question raised by my last letter. Sullen it may have been. Still, I want an answer. My dream did have an effect on me and, I must admit, on our controversy. I shan't tell you about it now, except to say that it raised all sorts of questions about that dream you had some years ago. You never told me much of that either. I wonder, was it as intensely personal as mine? I have decided that I won't share mine with anyone unless I come to understand it better myself. What would be the use? It would only make me look ridiculous for having given it ten minutes' thought. I have never in my life told a dream satisfactorily. I always find myself telling the parts I remember, then limping along behind the description with vague adjectives trying to shore up the force of it.

Perhaps you've had time to come to terms with yours by now. I'd like very much to have you share it if you feel you could. I think it might help me with all this.

Your brother,
Paul

Dear Paul,

Here's my dream. But a line or two for preface.
Your confessed predicament at trying to communi-
cate a dream is exactly mine. My description shall be
ploddingly linear, a string of events, a thin line, not
the violent gush of images, feelings, sensations which
it was. Thus most of the terror will be missing. I
doubt imagination, even yours, will be able to make
up the lack.

I stood before God.

Now I can't describe his face. (I had no desire to see
it.) But the voice I can tell you about . . . somewhat.
Perhaps you, too, have opened your eyes in the night
with a stark conviction that something awakened
you, some . . . sound. Only it died away just at that
moment when your wits collected themselves about
you. You even have an impression of the unheard
sound. It was sharp, a slap against a wall. Or it was
dull, a thud, a falling of some heavy thing onto a car-
peted floor. Or, perhaps, it was a small explosion, a
pistol shot, some concussive blast of air. Well, his
voice was like that. That is, the sound of it never
seemed to fall quite on the ear. It fell on something . . .
deeper in, vibrated across some inner hollow.

My audience with him was very brief and much
longer than I wanted. I say "audience" though I

didn't speak. He spoke. The phrase I remember was "Take it from him." And take it they did. It came off quickly and in such a manner that I marveled. I marveled to think that I once thought it was mine. In order to make sense of this I must digress and tell you about me, and, perhaps a little about you.

I shall begin with love. What a black alchemy we work with words. We say, "love is . . . " and then attach to it whatever superlatives we can think up: sublime; the deepest emotion; the ultimate experience. Then we say, "I love you." By such semantical magic we pronounce ourselves dancers in the highest dance we can imagine.

But who has not shied away from any close inspection of his own affections? What motives do we leave undisturbed beneath those dark seams for fear that what we thought (hoped? wished?) to be love was really something else. You love her. Do you now? And if her lovely face were torn by an accident, not merely marred, mind you, but transformed into a horror? And if a tumor pressed her brain, convulsing her genial manner into some permanent bitter temper? Do you love her? Or do you merely find her pleasing at the moment?

But there *is* something, you insist, some sustained impulse toward her good, toward her welfare. You know neither whence it came nor whither it goes. It is there. You find yourself incapable of denying it or of commanding it. Certainly you do not feel it for everyone. You find—literally find, discover—that it is there for her. And you are delighted. Remember the total euphoria when first you found it there?

But do you see? It is there. It happened to you, the songs all say. It's ebbing alarms you. It's return to higher tides relieves you. For how should you live without it?

Let me be sure it's clear. I speak not of another's love for you, now, but of your love for another: that lilting, joyful liberty to raise some interest above your own. How, indeed, should you live without that? Now, what if (as you might suspect if you dared) it were never yours to begin with? What if your capacity, your very ability, to love were never yours but loaned to you? Suppose the lender returned to ask an accounting. And then, unsatisfied, he took it back.

If we knew someone who couldn't love, not merely didn't, but couldn't, we would pity him, fear him, loathe him. We would shudder and turn away, pronouncing him dead though he lived.

So at his command they took it from me and shuddered and turned away. I cried out, "Oh, my God. No!" But it was already done.

In that first horrible moment alone (and I knew that I had never before been truly alone) I searched the tiny remainder, that irreducible sediment I could still call "me." Surely there was some loving I could keep. But I could not find the motive, Paul. I went through every possible object: my wife, my son, my brother, my friends, my dog. But when I reached, I reached into a hole, a vast and wintry blackness. Some unthinkable lobotomy had been done. I tried to remember, to conjure up the emotions that must have accompanied loving.

My only utterance may seem ludicrous. And perhaps it was only that—that peculiar, wild inconsistency that terrorizes our dreams. Yet, perhaps, it is precisely what one would utter and utter forever. "Oh, my God. No! Oh my God, no! Ohmygod, no! Ohmygodno!" I do remember saying it over and over and seem to remember saying it until I awoke. Perhaps it would become a chant, the meaning alternately lost in repetition and found again with renewed shivers of horror. But such oscillation I believe would imply the kind of numbness to pain which blesses only time. Eternity will probably suffer no such periodic attrition. Joy or horror, unmixed, will be always and fully present there, I expect.

Nor was loving all he took back. Courage. Does that surprise you? It did me, though it shouldn't have. You, of course, remember the close call with the mad dog when we were boys, how you came back and fought the mongrel off when I had fallen. But do you remember what you said? After we had laughed and cried and laughed some more, still trembling, you said with wonder in your voice: "I can't believe I really did that! I would have thought I'd run away!" Somehow, or even somewhere, you found the courage. Think of it. You found it. You neither knew where it came from or how long it stayed. It was given to you when you needed it.

Courage. Yes, and when they took that I don't like to tell you what I felt. Craven would be the adjective, I suppose. But it was a noun.

I remember asking you once if you could find it in your heart to forgive me for something (I've forgotten

Whatever you would call it—magnanimity, grace—you found it. Do you see? We could have known even then. That, I think, was what raised my sharpest howl of despair in the dream: that I could have known.

I could say more. But I think you'll see the rest for yourself. Have you read the Gospels? Do you recall the parable of the talents? If so, you'll remember that the fellow who did nothing with his was stripped of it. It was given to one of the others who'd used his well. If you don't remember all the specifics I'll bet you haven't forgotten the shocking words: ". . . but from him who has not, even what he has will be taken away."

I needn't labor the point that I did not feel like a man once all this was taken from me. How should I describe what I did feel myself to be? A little twisting worm? I don't know. But I can tell you this: I felt sep-arate—separate from everything, anything (anything else, that is). I was an inward turning thing endlessly turning inward upon itself and find-ing not quite nothing. For there was identity there: fear and greed and rage and hatred and resentment. It was fear and greed and rage and hatred and resentment mixed in such proportions as to be uniquely me. I recognized myself, and would have fled this old, well-known horror. But there was no fleeing it. Not anymore. Not ever.

Your brother,
Robert

Dear Dad,

Thank you for the invitation to bring Laura home.
But, well . . . the relationship seems to have been
built on sand after all. Your early warning about
foundations was wise and wasted.

One begins to understand what all those old poets
were moaning about: to live in the continual possi-
bility of seeing her; to know that she is alive and
moving within the same city; to know that
coincidence alone is lacking. And when you least
expect it, when, blissfully, you've forgotten to hope or
dread, a girl rises from a table across the room. It is a
rude jerk from dumb sleep. The heart starts a rough
rhythm; the breath is shortened. And none of this you
want. It is a torture. The girl has simply tossed her
hair in some disturbingly familiar way. Or is it the
merest similarity of some outer contour against the
light, the lines of the coat flowing from her shoulders?
Whatever. It passes quickly. The face is alien, a
cheat. It isn't her. But another morning is ruined;
another bad night is coming.

What buffoons we are to think we rule ourselves
with our minds. Mine has been giving unheeded lec-
tures to every other part of me, it seems, for a week.
My affections and my senses—these are already in
deep famine and will not sit still for any pedantic

wagging of the finger. But memory—to him they will listen, and rapt, too. Ah, and what an enchanter he is: teasing, baiting, elaborating. Like any good story-teller he tells the best ones over and over, embellishing, shamelessly, as he sees his listener's eyes growing wide, and in the end, reducing me, all of me, to an appetite, simple and ravenous . . . for her!

And a whimpering appetite it is at that. So here's the humor in it. I've become a sucker, Dad—I who hate melodrama—an easy mark, these days, for any sad song, any sentimental rhyme. The enclosed piece, "Explanation," will give you the idea I think. It's humiliating in the extreme. You'd have great fun with me if you were here. And I wish you were.

Your slow-learning son,
Jeff

Explanation

And when she said she'd leave—know what it's like
   to have the voice without the words to match?
That's why he cried like that, cried out
   almost without a word.
Just then he was at one with all
   the pain-racked animals he'd ever heard
who didn't even have the ugly guttural
   "No don't!" that he at least could say.

Dear Jeff,

I greatly enjoyed the lines about your hangover d'amour. See? Melodrama has its not unsubstantial pleasures. I was beginning to fear you would never discover them. For if they evade you while you are callow, what hope have you? And who would desire to miss such delicious misery?

And what a perfect time of year to be sentimental! Indeed, can anyone not be sentimental in autumn. I enclose "October," if not to cheer you, at least to get you a little more mileage from your mood.

With love,
Dad

October

So winter's won this war again
And summer's hapless troops
Lay down their leaves and droop their helmet plumes
Their fragrant trumpets mute at last
Their petal banners strewn across the cooling forfeit
ground
Submitting to the occupation hoarde
Already falling cold and white
To hold the conquered land in chilly thrall.

Now wait the pale insurgent roots
And tiny squalling seeds
Laid underground in battle haste
By dying mothers, hidden there against the day
When common cause can once again
Be made with the ascending sun
To drive the hated ice foe from the land
And lift again their bright flags in the air.

Dear Philip,

If we have our dates right you should be back at your desk by now. I hope the trip was successful. When and where should we look for the new article?

Maggie is still laughing at all the anecdotes you dug out (at my considerable expense). When I advise her that not one in three is true, she only says that if they didn't really happen they should have. So you've made a fan.

But say, did we detect in you something like a partisan against the women's movement? Your historic contempt for politics would have led me to believe such a stance unlikely. Still, you usually reserve your best humor for topics that truly interest you. Come clean, Mabry! If you take a side, let's see your flag in the open.

And listen, Philip, I have it on the highest authority (two on one) that you were with us when the birdshot flew at Huddleston's orchard. If you continue to deny it you shall have to take on Paul and perhaps the entire scientific community as well. For he may have hit upon a plan to link you quite scientifically to our folly in a way that will make all your denials utterly futile.

And I positively insist on being there when you eat your words. Don't start without me.

Yours in the right,
Robert

Dear Robert,

Well, I did ask for the dream. You were right. Most of the terror was gone (for all your eloquence). I will not be harried into the snare by such metaphysical frights as these. I hope your dream was not instrumental in your conversion. It would be a disappointment to know that you, of all people, gave in under such threatenings. Crude servility doesn't fit you.

I got a most curious letter from a publisher about my manuscript. To condense two single-spaced pages: "Yes. No. Well, maybe. Would you consider some major revisions?" My answer (made bold by your encouragements) was no—at any rate not until I've tried another publisher or two. And I think that's right. I'm no schoolboy ahungering to see my name in print. So it's off to another publisher.

Edith's not feeling well, and I'm playing nurse this week. So please excuse a short letter.

Love,
Paul

Dear Paul,

Yes, the dream was instrumental in my conversion; that is, it had its part in the long, slow process which took place in me. But it was only one of his arrows. There were many. As to the servility of fear as a motive, I have something to say.

When did you become so high minded? Do you remember when we struck up a fire on the hearth of that old shack in Shropshire and you sent me out after more wood? And when I rushed in to tell you that the old, tinder-dry roof had caught fire from the faulty chimney . . . well, as I remember, you had no scruples then about fear being a legitimate motive. Still, there in the burning hut you might have delivered the same pious lines you penned to me in the opening paragraph of your letter. They would have applied equally.

I know the objection forming in your mind: fleeing a burning building is different from flying into the arms of a powerful bully, promising to love and honor him if only he will not beat your very brains out. Well, it is a false picture produced chiefly, I think, by the very fear you speak of. Oh yes. It operates in you even if you think you refuse to submit to it. It has driven you to paint false pictures for yourself.

Of course you remember what we did after the

shack burned to the ground in view of almost everyone in the village! Neither of us shall ever forget the agony of hiding from Father. But it was you, Paul, who corrected my picture of our father that night. For my fear and guilt had conjured an image of him as a terror, a merciless avenger and, yes, a bully of sorts. Now I don't know if I really could have brought myself to run away. Thanks to you, I didn't try. You were older; you knew Father better. Oh, you trembled at first and even entered into my denunciations. It is painful to remember what general and specific injustices I accused Father of through the early hours of that night. Then, gently, you began to pour on your balm. "Surely we'll get a terrible flailing," you admitted, "I won't lie to you about that. But think, Bobby, then it'll all be over. He always takes us on his lap afterwards. And it'll all be over."

The point is this: it is possible to construe a person in total error out of fear and guilt. You see, fear had its part in our going home to face the music that night. For what should we have done otherwise? Run off to become Dickensian waifs? But it was your clear thinking and surer knowledge of Father, I think, that finally sent us back. Father was not a bully. The problem was of our own making. You showed me that, as no other person in the world could have, because he was your father, too, and because you shared my guilt.

Now, greatly multiply the offense, the guilt and the fear, and imagine what kind of picture you might paint of a father. Then let an older brother who was not in on the terrible deed at all come along and tell

43

you three things: first, he knows the father better than you, and you have painted a false picture for yourself; second, when you speak of running away, you have no conception of the horrors that you would be running away into; and third, he, the older brother, will go back with you, share your guilt and take your whipping.

Now, tell me just what proportion of servile fear would be involved in your response. Even so. To my knowledge, Jesus never quibbled with any motive that would, in fact, get the threatened one out of the burning hovel. IIe talks quite openly of rewards. Does that offend you too—a bit mercenary for your taste? Is it shameless bribery to promise that out there, out of the burning building, out of the blistering choking furnace, there is fresh, breathable air? Or, to reverse the image, I remember one incidental point you made to me in that long, cold night in the woods. "At least, it'll be warm at home." You could have gone on without me, but you appealed to every motive you could to persuade me to go, too. (Of course, some would say you simply didn't want to face Father alone. But I know you better than they.)

Sorry Edith is under. Nothing serious we hope?

I'm glad about your decision re the manuscript. I don't understand their response. If this is your statement, built up on years of work in the field, why would they want to put a different statement in your mouth? Minor revisions perhaps, but no, not major changes in a work of this kind.

With love,
Robert

Dear Dad,

First, thanks for "October." I think it's one of your best.

I confess to some of your charge. The lines about Laura did show a little luxury of self-pity. That is the damnation of the thing. Once one is dragged up there again (though I insist the trip is involuntary) one enjoys a bit too much the ride down into the next stupor. It is passing, but slowly. I have begun to look at other girls. Still, this one's too fat and that one's mind is too slow, this hair too coarse, that face too white. What else am I betraying to your penetrating eye? That her whole appeal was a bit low? But once the relationship, the higher communion, has gone sour, one is permitted, surely, to remember the pleasing color of the fruit or the very succulence, the texture. Hm?

They are afflicting us here with a fad and not even a current one. It's something called open space. This is an arrangement in which many classes are placed in a single, large room and there challenged to create whatever nonmaterial boundaries (for benefit of eye, ear and sanity) can be devised. The "room" (think of a large steno-pool) is deadened by various acoustical means so that the activities of different classes will not interfere with one another. However, care is said to be given that the room is not so dead as to prevent a teacher from being heard by his own students twenty feet away (a common problem in these arrangements, we are told).

A delegation from the central office was here last spring to ask whether we would like to have our conventional building thus transformed. They insisted that we not give an answer immediately but rather think about it and discuss it among ourselves. We insisted, however, on giving an immediate answer (a unanimous "no!" shouted almost in unison). They then said that our "top of the head" response would certainly, most certainly, be taken into consideration and with that they left the meeting. We knew that their visit was only a bureaucratic way of telling us what they were, in fact, going to do.

Their crews worked all summer and should have finished before school started. But "the sack of Carmody High" goes on at this very hour. The designation "fall term" has taken on a new meaning as the walls come down. We teachers huddle together, homeless amid the rubble, and watch the pillage with morbid interest. The one who's enjoying it is the ancient history teacher. He told me he jumped over Mesopotamia, Egypt and Greece and went right to the fall of Rome. This was an opportunity not to be missed, he said.

I have so far escaped the actual unwalling of my room. By a happy accident of geography it will be one of the last to go. My worst problem has been the ubiquitous pall of plaster dust. But even now the roar of their jackhammer is upon me.

morituri te salutamus,
Jeff

Dear Bobby,

You and your brother shall not prevail. The forces
of science, I assure you, are not easily harnessed in
the service of petty tyranny. I stand secure on my
dignity. I would never have been party to so larcenous
a scheme as you describe, and I have any number of
witnesses ready to swear to my whereabouts if you
will only be so kind as to give me the precise date in
question. I'm no quaking student at your mercy.
Whatever the totalitarian customs at that little
school where you teach, intimidation will not work
with me. Though you and Paul and all science and
the arts conspire against me, I stand upon the truth.
As to eating my words, I answer with "Hardly a
Threat" (enclosed).

It was very good to see you and Maggie. The dinner
was smashing. How you (and Paul) did so well in the
matter of mating, by the way, I shall never understand. If you ever run on to another woman anywhere
near the quality of Maggie or Edith, please notify me
immediately. I should, on evidence of that alone, be
persuaded to reconsider my celibate vows.

Ah yes, women . . . and their movement. I take no
side. I mostly have questions. I mostly have a question. Has no one ever noticed that there are demon-
strable anatomical differences between a male and a

female? My question is: what do these differences imply? The only answer I have ever heard is that they imply . . . nothing. Absolutely and consummately *nothing*! But the answer is given in such a nervous hurry that I begin to suspect something.

The plain fact is: there are differences which we can readily see. Now the plain question is: are there other differences we cannot see so readily? But the very volume level of all replies betrays something. The question itself has become the most intolerable heresy. In another age one could be burned at the stake for less. It is rather like the heresy (I wonder, do behaviorists know they have orthodoxies, doctrines to protect?) of suggesting that there may be, after all, notable differences among the races. And here, some have been burned at the academic stake. Alas, I partly cheered at the pyre, for I suspect some of the researchers' motives.

What I really wish is that someone could come up with insuperable evidence that any race is somehow and to any degree you wish (it wouldn't matter to me) superior to the Caucasoid. What great blaring trumpets I would blow! What free air I would breathe again! To think that in spite of the most closely guarded bastions of ecclesiastico-sociological excathedras (excuse my excesses, I become a fanatic) truth would out! What total euphoria! Nothing since Galileo would rival it for sheer unshackling. The fall of the Bastille—fah! What would that be in comparison? A mere freeing of bodies.

If someone were to ask the difference between my hand and my foot, and I were to reply with shrill insistence that there is no difference at all worth noting, I should surely be suspected of having some secret doctrine to protect.

Let us suppose the questioner, one of those exasperatingly cool and objective types, pressed the matter a bit.

"But they're designed differently. You see, take this one on the end of your leg, here . . . "

"No, no," I reply peevishly. "See? There is a thumb on both of them, and four fingers!"

"Do you often walk on your hands, then?" he might ask.

"From time to time," I would say, "it makes no difference. Hands and feet both do all jobs equally well. Whichever of them happens to be closest to the ground in any given instance is the thing I walk on."

"Very interesting," he might say. But I think he'd say something else as I moved away, awkwardly, on one hand and a foot.

So, except for the issue of intellectual freedom, I am afraid I have very little interest in the developments beyond the great comic implications. If people want to walk upon hands, or upon a tongue and one ear, it makes no difference to me. I should rather enjoy the show.

But let's see your flag on the matter.

Your friend,
Philip Mabry

P.S. Eagerly I await the inevitable piece of civil rights legislation which makes it unlawful to refuse a man admittance as a patient in the maternity ward of a hospital solely on the ground of his sex.

Hardly a Threat

I'd love to sink my teeth into a succulent or two
  Be pleased to plop a plump into my cheek
I crave to crush my cuspids cross a crunchy clutch of crisp
  Suck on sour sweetly, so to speak
I'll eat flavor off the floor, float to Flanders on a barge
  if the chance of finding fresh there isn't even very large
When you say I'll eat my words, what a lovely thing to say
  Help me get this napkin on, can I start then right away?

Dear Jeff,

About open space: I see that it is possible to conduct classes under such conditions, but what is the point of deliberately creating handicaps? Is it the sheer challenge which they relish? "Just think what an accomplishment it would be if students could actually learn and teachers could actually teach in such an environment!" Something like that perhaps?

For pure bureaucratic daring your people rival our own here. We have a rule in the arts and sciences school that I only recently discovered. The effect of it is this: if a student makes an F, he can take the course over and replace the bad mark with a better one which he may earn on the second try. If, however, he makes a D it will stand. He may take the course over as many times as he likes, but the original sorry mark will not be expunged till rivers run uphill.

Consider the effect this must have on some student whose grade teeters between C and D. If he is of the dicier sort he may elect to see the course through, risking the indelible D. If he has no taste or talent for gambling, he'd better, in all prudence, cave in and go for the F.

Now if a committee of six, endowed with a generous stipend, were to sit at a table all day, every day, for a period of three months with no other business before it than the design of a single rule capable of completely unnerving a certain proportion of anxious sophomores and sending them home, blithering, to their mothers, I say they could not have done better than this! Bravo!

In sympathy,
Dad

Dear Philip,

I should have known you'd turn the question back on me. The truth is I don't see how to enter the general debate on the women's movement. No. I go further than that. I don't see how Christians can well enter into the general debate on social issues at all. Now it is possible to try, and some do. But all of us have trouble with it.

The trouble is that we have become accustomed to having the benefit of an outside Opinion on everything that matters to us. But . . . you see, this particular opinion is disallowed in the debate. In fact, the moment you mention it you are met with slack-jawed stares as if you'd said something (a) unfair (b) outrageous or (c) patently childish and illogical. "Look, if you can't play by the rules . . . " the silence says.

Now I suppose we could play by those rules, but it's hard to get interested in such an artificial exercise. Most social issues are too important to treat so academically. We recommend seeking real answers to the questions even if it means getting Advice.

Truly yours,
Robert

Dear Dad,

I can't answer your questions about open space any more than I can answer my own. I asked the principal proponent from the central office, "What's it for?" He went on rather grandly about how it affords us the ability to use space creatively. I said yes, but how? As far as I can make out he has only one example: "Well, let's say you want to show a film to three or four classes at once. This way there's no need to move the students to an auditorium. You simply make a slight rearrangement of the furniture and do it right here in your area." I replied that, yes, that might happen four or five times a year. How else is this space to be creatively used? He laughed, paternally, and said, "Why, the ways it can be used are limited only by your imagination." Yes, and his.

I have heard one other justification, on slightly less idealistic grounds. It is cheaper than a building "honey-combed with little cubicles." True. But to tear those expensive walls out once they are blissfully there! We need a Joseph Heller here. I haven't the talent to portray this sublime stupidity in all its reverberating splendor. Our wing looks like a temporary school set up in a mammoth train station during a civil disaster. Mental concentration in such a controlled riot is nearly impossible. I don't know which noise is worse, the visual or aural. Oh yes. They have a "quiet room" for children who simply flip out in the pandemonium. It is (need I say) the most popular area in the building.

They promise us that after a while the students will no longer be so distracted. Presumably, their questing eyes and minds will learn to shut out everything, including their teachers.

"But why?" I think I shouted. "Would you like to have your office out here in this anthill? Well, would you?"

At this question he smiled again. "It'll work out. You'll like it, I promise you, once you're used to it."

The image I could not escape, at that moment, was the one on the last page of Orwell's *1984* where Winston suddenly realizes that he loves Big Brother as the bullet plows softly into his brain.

Laura dropped by today. Just like that. I routinely answered a knock and there was thunder and lightning framed in the door, pretending to be a mere girl. She came in and sat on my sofa and drank my coffee and spoke trivial words into my ears and stood up and went away, leaving me to do whatever I could without her again. What is this? I thought I was normal again. She must have sensed, this enchantress, that the spell needed a little propping up.

She's gaining weight, though. Heh, heh.

So now I know. Whatever it was, it was not quite love. Not so strong a thing as love. I want to know that she's unhappy as well, that she's under my spell, too. This is terrible. What a bundle of itches and aches and hungers I am. Yech! God deliver.

Your son,
Jeff

Dear Bobby,

Oh yes, the Christian thing would dictate your position. And, of course, it would be deadly serious. Never have I encountered anything which emits such unrelieved gravity as your religion. And it runs right through to the heart. I've read the Gospels. Where are the jokes, Bobby? It's not natural. What other lubricant than humor is sufficient for the daily abrasion of living. Indeed, I either treat this seventy- or eighty-year span as a joke (perhaps a bad one, or more precisely, one in bad taste) or I go mad.

So I laugh at you all—you, the feminists, the vegetarians, the teetotalers and such like. I'm quite certain that the only ones who are safe in laughing at sacred cows are those of us whose cow is humor itself. And we may laugh with impunity. I defy you to make fun of humor.

Yours laughing,
Philip

P.S. To document all this I cite "Free Lesson" (enclosed). It actually happened to me! I walked on air for a week. As farce, it was perfection.

Free Lesson

They bend their heads together beside the fern.
The young one looks as eager as I to learn
the secrets of the masters hanging here.
I must get close enough to this to hear.
I do—in time to hear the old one say,
"Turn at Matisse, then first door past the Monet."

Dad,

I'm all excited about a discovery I made this morning, and it won't wait till next week's letter: a day is made up of seasons! Perhaps every other person in the world has noticed this. Nevertheless, for me, it lit this commonplace day with small wonders. I even made a little rhyme of it.

Seasons of the Day

A day has its own seasons
   Morning is its spring
To melt the tiny winter
   Night must always bring
And afternoon is summer
   Ripening on its way
To evening, little autumn
   Harvest of the day.

And, the more I think on it, the less it seems a forced analogy. I've learned not to be surprised in this. Nature is so unspeakably rich in fullness and in reverberations and echoes of herself that we have dug for a hundred generations and not come to the end of her.

When I was a boy I could never get a toy real enough. If it was a truck, I wanted the hood to open. And then there must be a motor inside. The motor must then run. And a driver must be there and he must be able to move and, preferably, talk and think. Imagine the frustration of finding only an undifferentiated chunk of plastic where there should have been pistons and valves, moving and messy and making small noises. (I wouldn't dare tell this childish wish to some. They would have *me* filled with Freudian plastic stuff. No such theory could be sufficient. The persona is just as richly dense with layered reality as any other part of nature.)

There are no undifferentiated chunks of plastic in nature. In fact, those who study her most deeply tell us we have only begun to discover the vastness of our ignorance about her complexity. We thought we'd found the chunks in atoms. Then in the nucleus and the electron. But there are (I am told), within all these, whole little worlds and within those, quarks! I think "quark" is a kind of code word (coined in frustration perhaps) for certain unexplained phenomena, kinks in the theory. I love the word. I can hear it.

"Quark, quark . . . quark, quark, quark."

"Oh, shut up," science says, "no need to rub it in."

"Quark." (He quarks best who quarks last.)

Yours,
Jeff

Dear Jeff,

Bravo your "Seasons of the Day." There is at least one other person in the world to whom the idea had never occurred.

Your thoughts on nature coincide with a train of thought set off in me by a friend the other day. God could have given us water in some serviceable prosaic form, but simple utility was not enough for him. He is Jesus, the generous, pouring out upon us such an extravagant profusion of sensual beauty in clouds and snow and mist and dew, and icicles and rainbows and waterfalls and raindrops, in brooks that trickle, and rivers that roll and breakers that roar—until, overwhelmed, we almost forget that the diaphanous and iridescent stuff will, by the way, quench our thirst and clean our hands and cool us when we're hot.

And shall we forget fire and color and music and beasts and foliage and good black earth? The same hand is recognized in all. So we sit back and join our fingertips in thoughtful meditation, speculating that if God doesn't particularly like beauty, perhaps he doesn't mind it. Indeed! He thought it up! He is the maker of delights. We are the shriveled ascetics.

And is it any wonder that pantheism erupts out of rebellion? One may refuse to obey God, but who can resist his artistry? Who could fail to worship something when placed within such an atmosphere? But those who are tempted to make nature a goddess should take note that she, for all her wonder, was made in six days only. When Jesus left the upper room to die, he said he was going to prepare a place for those who love him. What if he has spent the whole two thousand years making that place? If so, I think this present six-day wonder will, by comparison, seem to be a minor work of the artist, or more likely, the first rough sketch of a masterpiece.

I dare not say *the* masterpiece for who knows what other things he does. "The secret things belong to God." We know for sure that he is unsearchable, that we shall never come to the end of him. I think your quarks shall be long understood and explained as to babes in the nursery before we know all the forms, even, of God's art, much less the mighty works themselves. I fancy the gallery is literally endless to display the works of him who by the word of his mouth calls things into being which were not.

With love,
Dad

Dear Robert,

All right. I think it's time we had this out. You said your dream was only "one of his arrows" or something to that effect. Well, in God's name, what were the rest? How have we ended up so far apart? Am I a wicked man because I can't believe, damned because I can't operate against the evidence I have? Was it Mark Twain who said, "Faith is believing what you know ain't so?" Well, is that it? If it is, then please admit it. If not, then tell me what it *is*. Because from here it looks for all the world as if you've joined in to praise the emperor's new clothes.

Edith is a little better but the problem is stubborn. Something about the colon. The doctor speaks of surgery, but we've decided to ride it out a bit longer. Still, our household's a mess. I've no talent at any of the jobs required to keep the thing running.

Affectionately,
Paul

Dear Dad,

Your letter about the generosity of creation arrived today and with exquisite timing. I was in one of those sloughs where all God's words look like restraints. "Thou shalt not" was loud and everywhere. I had forgotten that the negative is necessary to shape the positive. What the sculptor takes away is as important as what he leaves, isn't it? If he didn't restrain some of the stone (chip it away) there would be no sculpture. And, as so often happens, once I noticed the principle of "*this* not that," I began to see it everywhere.

In a TV screen, I am told, each tiny dot has all colors potentially present. The reds and greens are restrained here and we have blue. Over there the red and blue are held back and we see green. Cast away all restraint, use every potential hue at every point and we have nothing—a blank white glare.

A chef is careful to measure: only this half teaspoon of cinnamon and no more. Is his art chiefly devoted to teasing us with condiments? Why not dump in the whole box? Think what cookery would be without restraint.

God says no because of the yes he is doing. I was so taken up with the material on the sculptor's floor (all that gorgeous marble wasted) that I hadn't looked at

the work itself—the mighty yes he was making.
I've tried for it in "Warrior-Smith." Will it do?

Love,
Jeff

Warrior-Smith

Laid on that unyielding anvil of his
  And hot from the forge of his eye
Malleable under his hammers at last
  My stubborn misshape has to die

Beating and pounding, relentless he plies
  The blows, in thunder they fall
Tonging me, holding me, not letting go
  When, glancing, I run from his maul

Plunging me under the icy bath
  I seethe in the bubbling steam
Tempered, annealed, to see if I'll bend
  He flexes me over a beam

Fingers the line where he'll lay on my edge
  His stone is so hard on my steel
Grinding, remorseless, he wears me away
  Till dullness is gone on his wheel

Lovingly laid on the flat of his thigh
  Anointed with pumice and oil
Burnished and polished until I reflect
  His own image, perfect and loyal

Turning me slowly before his regard
  He celebrates what he has made
Out of a lifeless, awkward iron
  A slender and lissome blade

Holding me, weighing me in his hand
  He tries me—I flash through the air
Sheathing me, hanging me light on his hip
  Right ready, he carries me there

Dear Jeff,

I like "Warrior-Smith." The last two stanzas are
the best for me. Some lines gave me trouble (first
stanza, fourth line is difficult; second stanza "relentless" is just a little weak, same with "flash" in the
last stanza), but taken together I think it works
fairly well. Keep it up!

As to "restraint," I'm with you. It is necessary but
not, by a long chalk, is it the main theme. If it were,
one could imagine an alternative approach to the
creation. Think of nature in the hands of an efficiency-
minded administration. Grapes would certainly not
ferment in such a nature, nor would sound (such a
good useful tool) ever be allowed to soar into the frills
of music. And flowers, if we must have them for the
bees, could all be given some sturdy uniform color.
And why do we need more than one variety, by the
way? Such incautious prodigality! Then, of course,
every flower and every bee must learn to attend to
duty more assiduously. All those frivolous blossoms,
those whose nectar never makes its way into the
honey at all, must be brought to account. And, now I
think of it, why do we need honey? Anyone would
think we were running this system for fun! Better to
do away with flowers altogether . . . *and* bees. Good
sensible economy must be brought into play at some

point. Here is the perfect place to trim the budget. Yes . . . and *trees*! Oh, of course, we all like to spend, spend, spend! But frills are, after all, frills, and we can't have everything, can we?

Perhaps vegetation itself could be rethought. I see no reason why a simple standardized mat of—but here! Do we really need anything of this sort at all? Minerals are really quite serviceable. Of course, even they are wastefully diverse. I see no excuse for such immoderate gaudiness as gold *and* marble *and* amethyst *and* quartz! Spend, spend, spend! Now you take brimstone. There's a practical rock! I see no reason why we couldn't simply. . . .

It is not God who designed the reductive ideal of nirvana. I make it a far cry from there to the gleaming city of God replete with jeweled foundations, great pearl gates, crystal river, tree of life, fruit. . . . Surely heaven's delights are more articulate than earth's. Certainly not less.

Our love to you,
Dad

Dear Paul,

It was a pleasure to talk to you on the phone even under such circumstances. Any change in Edith's condition? Maggie is skeptical about your temporary maid being able to handle the situation. I chide her that she never expects anyone else can do a thing as well as she can. (Is Edith like that?) Still, it's all I can do to keep her from packing her bags.

If the maid doesn't work out, promise that you'll call. Maggie would be a lot happier there, doing something, than she is here, stewing. Keep us informed.

Now for the question raised by your letter: how did I come to faith?

You remember what fun Mabry had convincing me (I must have been all of five years old) that the trees were really great sorcerers who flung the wind from their fingertips. I can still recreate in my mind the solemn resonance in his young voice (he couldn't have been more than eight) as he let me in on this deep secret of the ages. Well, I must now confess to you (don't tell Philip) that I no longer believe it. I have come to believe something else: it is the trees that are acted on by the wind.

Now. How did this wind faith come about in me? When, when precisely, did I arrive at my present belief that something unseen (wind) causes something seen (tree movement)? Can I demonstrate, demonstrate unanswerably, that it is wind that moves the trees? What first convinced me? And what if I were to discover that the early logic which led me to wind faith was faulty? Would I then be compelled to return to the Mabry tree faith? Is our view of reality conditioned on the logic by which we first arrived at it? I say no.

Truth is I don't *know* how I arrived at wind faith or when. I don't remember. Is it important? It is not that arrival, it is the accumulation of evidence since the arrival that makes the tenet more or less unshakable.

Listen, Jesus said a helpful thing: "Even though you do not believe me, believe the works, that you may know and understand that the Father is in me and I am in the Father."

Believe that you may know. Seem backward? Well, there it is. There is no way to know without believing. (Is it so strange, really? Don't scientists hint at this with their celebrated method: assume a theory is true, then set about to prove it. I don't suggest that hypothesis is very much like faith. My point is that it is no less backward in its approach.) This is why apologetics is so difficult for Christians. There is no good way to explain this house to you, or even to convince you beyond doubt that it is here, until you come in through the door.

"What door?" you may even ask.

"Look," I answer, "there's a door here—here, right *here*. Believe me; walk through it."

"How silly I would feel walking through a door I can't see," you say. Yes, I give you that. You may feel silly.

People walk in for all kinds of reasons, many of which you would find unacceptable; but in they come, and then they know. Jesus doesn't require a very high faith to begin. The quantity or quality of faith is secondary to the act itself. Believe only in the works themselves if you must, he says. Listen to something from John's Gospel, "Now when he was in Jerusalem at the Passover feast, many believed in his name when they saw the signs which he did; but Jesus did not trust himself to them, because he knew all men and needed no one to bear witness of man; for he himself knew what was in man." You see? Jesus knew this wasn't a very advanced faith. But it was a start. The patriarch Abraham himself (who is held out as a paragon of faith) was said to have progressed from faith to faith.

Think of a thread tied to a rope tied to a brick. You can't pull the brick by the thread. But you can use the thread to pull the rope to your hand. And with the rope you can move the brick.

If you quiz people about why they are Christians you will likely concentrate on how they made their decision. This will frustrate you unless you understand it may not be their conversion experience that convinces them. What convinces them is what they found when they (for whatever reasons) believed. The cause for belief is probably peculiar to each person. You must get beyond that to find what is really common to Christians: the "know and understand" that Jesus promises.

There is no getting around this. He was speaking of "inside knowledge." I know well how hateful that term is to outsiders. It nearly drove me to rage. I thought believers to be unbearably smug and casual about apologetics. After all, since their whole faith rested on it (or so I thought), they might well re-examine their reasons for believing in the first place. None of them seemed very interested in doing that. It seemed that many of them had even forgotten why they first believed. Or worse, some even admitted that their original belief was circumstantial or accidental (family tradition, etc.). I attributed this unwillingness to re-examine their original belief to insecurity, but I see now why they didn't have much interest in the exercise.

I'm not sure if I can reconstruct for you (indeed, for myself) my original rationale for belief. It's like trying to remember precisely why I decided to marry Maggie. I'm sure there were reasons sufficient for me at the time (there must have been, I did it!), but they are not the reasons I would choose the same course today. But in neither case would my present reasons have been available until I'd stepped inside.

It began, I suppose, when I met this girl in a Chaucer class. She was a completely exasperating person. We studied together a few times, and when I asked her out she refused on the outrageous grounds that I was not a Christian. Here began my experience as an outsider. As a consolation, however, she invited me to a meeting of a little Christian group on campus, where I met others of this breed. Here began a two-year, running argument with a small set of people whose lives I admired, but whose philosophy seemed . . . well, stunted.

With them everything began and ended with Jesus. At first I thought them stupid, then ignorant, then deluded, then incomprehensible. But I could not escape a vague sense that there was something going on in them and among them. It was another encounter with trees bent by an unseen wind.

To shorten a long tale, they tried all their arguments on me—none of them very compelling. Somehow the whole of what they were was larger than the sum of what they said. I quit them finally, resigned to the fact that whatever it was they were describing, I was outside of it and not likely to find a way in.

A few years later I abruptly began thinking about it again. In the interim I had laid it aside as a quaint sophomoric preoccupation, a jumble of unanswerable questions. But during that interval I had taken a wife. And when that wife announced to me, one night in bed, that she had become a Christian, I groaned, rolled over and, quite unwillingly, reopened the subject. For the next six or eight months I drove poor Maggie to the wall two or three times a week. She could never satisfy me about her reasons for believing in Jesus. Fortunately for me, she didn't try. She would answer my questions as best she could and leave it at that. But there were certain changes in her life which indicated that that same unseen wind was stirring in my own house.

Well, I bought myself the best modern translation of the New Testament I could find and decided to face this Jesus head on once and for all and make an end of it. I thought if I could flush him from the thickets of antique language I might be at a better advantage. The results were inconclusive.

Though the poetic diction of the King James scholars was gone, there was something left that was extraordinary. Jesus seemed to speak paradox every time he opened his mouth, but it was clearly not double talk. He was not trying to confuse me. He seemed to know something that I didn't. I remember thinking to myself something like the following.

Suppose I knew about a whole realm of experience which my pupils had never had. What would I do? How would I, for example, explain music to a deaf student or color to a blind one. I concluded that I would have to go to analogy. This is exactly what I found Jesus doing. Metaphor and parable comprised a large part of his repertoire.

So I began to be a little easier on Jesus' teachings. Where I had earlier grumbled that the man would never give a straight answer to anything, I now began to concede that, well, after all, perhaps he couldn't. How would I have answered the deaf student who demanded a straight answer to his question: "What, in plain English, is this music you speak of?" If, in addition, the student was suspicious that such a thing really didn't exist at all, my attempted explanation might seem quite evasive.

About here, then, came my dream. Its main effect was counter-anesthetic. Our lives are anesthetized by routine, aren't they? Each morning, hardly ever realizing it, we remember who we are, how we fit into the world, etc. Rationally, we know that this present little groove of routine will not last forever. One day something will stop it. It may be that we will lose our jobs. Perhaps we will contract a terminal disease. Or someone else upon whom our routine depends will leave or change or die. At the very least, we will die. Rationally, we know that some radical change will occur sooner or later. Emotionally, however, we function as if this present routine of our life were essentially eternal. The more secure and stable our life, the more powerfully this anesthesia works. But occasionally we are jolted out of our little groove—a near disaster, someone's death, something will stubbornly hold our faces to the truth about our mutability. It may take a few minutes or a few weeks to shake it off and return to "reality" (unreality), but we will have been reminded, nevertheless, that what is now will not always be. In times of great and sustained risk, say battlefield conditions, people are often out from under the anesthesia for days or weeks at a time.

I don't know how they work for you, but dreams are often effective for me as de-anesthetizers. For a little while they function as an alternate reality. They remind me that much of what I consider real is only my personal milieu constructed and maintained to make my life emotionally bearable.

So, coming at a time when all this Christianity business was still safely intellectual and speculative for me, the dream simply threw me out of the rut for a bit and jarred my imagination loose. What if, in fact, there were a God who would demand an accounting from me. That would have been an intellectual image before, dry and abstract. Suddenly it was an emotional image. A sort of mental aberration, you'll say, an emotional (like an optical) illusion. Exactly. But the blow fell when, next day, I realized that my own secure and stable image of my existence was every bit as much an emotional illusion as my dream. What seemed flint-hard reality in my life was in fact supported by the thinnest eggshell of happenstance—as long as my heart continued beating (and why should it go on and on indefinitely as it seemed to be doing); as long as nothing went very wrong with the whole delicate mechanism which I call my body; as long as nothing went very wrong with the whole delicate mechanism which we call the economy, or the one we call society and so on. How tenuous my "real world" was! Of course, the pressure of the·ordinary—the morning newspaper, the weekly faculty meetings, the familiar places and faces and duties—all this made any vision of my own apocalyptic judgment seem quite remote. But judgment seemed no more remote than my own death. And since I knew for a rational fact that I was going to die, that sense of remoteness, of farfetchedness had to be disallowed as evidence for the first time in my life. I'd have to find some other reason to disbelieve in God or in judgment. No longer could I depend on the argument that it merely seemed unreal or unlikely.

So that was the main effect of the dream. And this was reinforced at the time from the most unlikely source you can imagine.

One night when Maggie's two little nephews were visiting we played Monopoly. Early on I happened into a monopoly of the railroads. I had always been rather contemptuous of the railroads, feeling them to be small-time, pocket-change affairs barely better than the water works. But this homely investment turned out to be the foundation on which I built a wildly successful empire. In an hour I was the scourge of the board. All dreaded my hotels.

When it became hopeless for the others, we declared the game at an end. The boys went off to prepare for bed, Maggie began doing something in the kitchen, and I took it upon myself to put the game away. As I sat sorting the money by denominations, something curious happened: the value of those colored, numbered sheets of paper evaporated, as it were, before my eyes. A few moments earlier that tidy stack of five-hundred-dollar bills had given a sense of security and well-being. Now it was nothing. The other players, the poor bankrupt things, had doubtless already forgotten their very bankruptcy. The real world was a relief to them. It *welcomed* them back. I, however, was suffering a sense of loss! It was the suddenness, I think. In the wink of an eye it didn't matter how much money or property I had, how cleverly I had gotten it, how little they had, how desperate they had been. I swept my houses and hotels off the board (in another round I would have owned everything from Virginia Avenue to Marvin Gardens, fully half the board and bristling with improvements) and, when everything was put away under the lid, it was just as if my wealth and success had never been. I was back now in a world of harder coin.

What would it be like if the *world* were folded like a garment and put away in a box, if all my carefully garnered wealth (my learning, my possessions, my achievements, alliances, plans) were thoughtlessly tossed away into a pile somewhere apart from me and I were left to stand—a naked spirit—in a different world of very hard currency indeed. Perhaps at that point I would notice that some of the players were overwhelmed with relief. Yes. Of course. They were those luckless bankrupt types who seemed less and less attentive to the game in those last few rolls, who kept looking away from the board to my great exasperation. Remember how I used to reprove them. "Pay attention to the game!" I would say.

But all this merely set the stage. I hadn't been convinced of the truth of the Christian position. I had only seen how flimsy was my defense against it. I had to admit that Christianity wasn't any less likely than many things which I didn't question. The road from there on into the kingdom is the most difficult for me to reconstruct. Most influential I think was the growing pressure of inference, that something, though unseen, was bending those trees. It wasn't just Maggie or the kids I'd met in the campus group. I seemed to keep encountering all kinds of evidences which, while not separately conclusive, taken altogether mounted like water against a dike.

Well, I plugged holes in the dike of my unbelief until I ran out of fingers. Just where did it start to crack? I don't know. I knew it was leaking too fast. I felt water in my shoes. Then my ankles were wet. The specifics probably aren't very important because everything that convinced me, put together and recounted to you with perfect accuracy would not, I think, convince you. I don't know what it would take to convince you. I doubt if you even know.

Really, Paul, I think it's impossible to understand all this, let alone believe it—without help. St. Luke's Gospel: "In that same hour [Jesus] rejoiced in the Holy Spirit and said, 'I thank thee, Father, Lord of heaven and earth, that thou hast hidden these things from the wise and understanding and revealed them to babes. . . .' " Do you see? God makes certain that all this is impenetrable to us until we'll come to him as babes. There's no question of our finding out. It has to be revealed. Lay aside your own wisdom and understanding and ask him to show you. Become a child before him. Do it, Paul.

Yours,
Robert

Dear Robert,

Edith is dramatically improved. We changed doctors (thanks to your urging) right after your phone call. This new one seems to know what he's doing and all thoughts of surgery are forgotten. We're keeping the maid for another week, but Edith is already feeling spunky enough to complain that it isn't necessary.

But, about your letter, you've certainly got me intrigued. What is this mysterious secret knowledge which one gets only after suffering the initiation rites? And all this "if only you'll step inside" business sounds . . . well, I think I've heard it somewhere. Isn't it what the spider said to the fly?

You, of course, remember Bruce Stidham. Did I tell you his wife died some time ago? He was by earlier in the week, and he's just now called again. I think his mind is at the snapping point with grief and loneliness. You wouldn't know him, Robert. "They Said a Year" is my attempt to fight off my own depression about him.

Paul

They Said a Year

They said to wait a year. He's waited two
and still apart from her
his life's a fever dream.
Oh, when can I wake up, he asks,
and find you here with me again
fitly curled against this hungry skin?
The news is sudden every morning in his half-full bed,
hot and hurting, blunt and unexplained: she's dead.

Dear Philip,

I think you have me. I've no idea how to make fun of humor! But I take seriously your questions about the lack of it in the Gospels and I'll try to give you a serious answer. Frankly, Philip, I've struggled with some of the same questions, myself.

Jesus, his teachings, his personality, all that we know of him from the Gospels has, for me, an unmistakable "feel" of life. It transposes into a new key what we already know, all our rock-bottom experiential knowledge. If there were another kingdom, one which fulfilled all the good dreams of the one we're in, surely Jesus would be its emissary. However, for me there was one curiosity, one chord that did not seem to transpose. That chord was humor. Why, indeed, did Jesus seem to emit such an unrelieved gravity?

I found exceptions in the Gospels, of course, but they seemed thinly scattered and trivial. In life as we know it, humor seems to be ubiquitous, as you well put it, the lubricant which makes bearable the daily abrasion of living. Beyond that, laughter often crowns the best moments of our lives. Is there no laughter where Jesus came from? I suspect now that it, or something better, is seldom absent from there. But I didn't come to that until I had thought a bit about humor itself.

Humor will not bear vivisection. The knife slays the joke. The thing "strikes" us funny or it doesn't. And when it strikes it ignores any conscious processing we might wish to do. All of us have laughed at things we wished weren't funny. And worse still is trying to laugh at something that isn't. We never are allowed to decide if a thing is funny. We're seldom able, even after the fact, to understand precisely why it was.

However, while any real analysis is unlikely, all who laugh know they laugh at very different kinds of things. There is laughter that wells up out of joy: the laughter of newlyweds or of old friends reunited. There is the laughter of parents at their two-year-old or of children with puppies. Then there is flippancy, derision, ribaldry and a special kind of laugh that erupts when justice is fitly served, a comeuppance received. But the categories become ragged, overlapping and insufficient. The point is that humor is not a thing but a rather loose name which we give to a whole lot of things. Sense of humor, what makes one laugh, is perhaps no more isolated a characteristic than what makes one cry: indeed some things (happiness, embarrassment) may trigger either laughter or tears on any given occasion. And, of course, laughter may proceed from great bitterness and be as painful as crying.

So, the question of why there is not more humor in Jesus or in Scripture may have to be recast. Is there humor there and, if so, what kind? I found that in my own search through Scripture for the thorny locust (the joke itself) I had neglected to notice that I was in a vast forest of giant sequoias. For Scripture is full of rejoicing. Quite frequently I was met by great knee-slapping shouts of joy. And if they have that there (in that other country) . . . well . . . would we not seem a bit crabbed to interrupt those shouts with our question: "But do you not make jokes here?"

And the locust is thorny. What you and I miss most in the Gospels, I think, is that special kind of humor (can we call it comic relief?), that running banter which slips through the crannies of the day. It is the lubricant you spoke of and it seems so often to turn on predicament or frailty or even wickedness. And it is often very productive, most of all when it provides relief from one's own ridiculousness. If it does its work well, it causes a healthy recoil from something unendurable in ourselves. Nevertheless, it is frequently humor in a minor key. There is a negative twist to it.

It is possible that Jesus used humor like this and it was simply not recorded. Perhaps it was considered less important than the kind of things which were recorded. It seems likely, however, that if it were pervasive it would have seeped in, if not in incident, at least in tone. My guess is that it was conspicuously absent. I am best able to imagine the absence in the context of a parable. Let me draw it in some detail.

I have just finished an extraordinarily good dinner at a friend's. We ate on his terrace with stars, lilacs, and the laughter and conversation of friendship. There was the best wine, crisp salad and a generous slice of beef. There was good coffee and good music.

Suddenly, I am called away from the table and given surprising news: as a result of my unceasing plea, I have by some caprice been granted, on this notice, to go immediately to the king's deepest dungeon to visit my son. I go at once. Behind a malevolent jailer and in the flickering light of his torch, I descend into the thick stale air (if one can call it air), down one long stair after another, level beneath level, and arrive at the place. The door is pried open with the greatest difficulty, and I wade into the cell, ankle deep in a mixture of water and accumulated human waste. There I find my son, my dearly loved and only child.

We cry, of course, and then we talk. Miraculously, I contain my emotion sufficiently to form thoughts in my brain and words on my lips. We talk of his captivity, of ways to allay his suffering, of the world I have just come from and most of all, of ways to get him out. Let him relieve his own misery if he can by a passing joke about the rotted bread which floats in his gruel. Let him laugh, if it will help, about the stench and about the maggots, and about how time flies when one is having fun.

Now—I will talk with him, I will cry with him, I will console him, I will suffer for him, indeed, I will take his place if they will let me. I will do anything my love for him can accomplish. But let him not, at such an hour, expect humor from me.

Absence of a sense of humor is usually taken as a defect in personality. We think he who has none a mutation. But if we see a man pressed by an urgent and serious mission, say an ambulance driver transporting the suffering victims of a terrible accident, we do not look for his humorous side during that time. In fact, at such a time we may think him seriously flawed if he does show it. If the period of time is protracted, we might forgive a need for the relief of some small humor, but if his laughter reveals an indifference to the gravity of the situation, that would be inexcusable.

Jesus' sense of urgent and serious mission is not difficult to find in the Gospels. "I have a baptism to be baptized with and how constrained I am until it is accomplished." How great was that constraint? A visit to the dungeon or a job driving an ambulance might exempt us from humor for a few hours. But what of three years? Yet, I think we could excuse a new arrival at Buchenwald if he did not laugh for some extended period—a few days, say, or even a few weeks. Are we too dull to extrapolate further, to imagine an outrage so massive that its very presence would pre-empt laughter for three years or even for a lifetime? But we have difficulty imagining a life without attrition, a life without the inevitable wearing down of resistance. We cannot conceive of a man going for three years without yielding to the need for comic relief. But, of course, the claim of the Gospels is that Jesus is unique.

So if this kind of humor was absent (and we can't be sure that it was) then I think it likely that, coming from his Father's table, where there was true laughter, unsullied by any negative cant, Jesus found our humor insipid or warped. If you had children whose sense of humor was chiefly expressed by tormenting a defenseless, crippled child, what course should you take? You could ignore it. You could enter into their "fun" and give the victim a blow or two yourself. Or you could tell the children that their sense of humor was crude and then try to elevate their taste. If you loved them very much, however, you might see their amusement as some warped outgrowth and set aside the whole subject of humor until you were able to get at the roots of their cruelty and wickedness.

In Jesus' kingdom we might well stand unamused in the presence of real humor with our eyes darting in embarrassment, searching for some key to the laughter. Nor would the key be available without some radical change in ourselves. Then, of course, we would need no key, our laughter being spontaneous. The lack of a sound sense of humor would be one of the minor discomforts of being suddenly thrust into that place unchanged. The music would likely din our ears and the light would probably strike us blind. Heaven is not a reward for good deeds. It is a place prepared for people who have undergone a certain kind of change.

For those who will not submit to the change, Jesus said there will be a different place. And if there is some counterpart to humor there, some leering smirk, some malignant sneer, then humor will be seen to be neither good nor bad, but rather an effusion, a stream revealing the character of its source.

Trapped here in this present life, however, in this bad joke as you say, I think we can only guess at real humor. Perhaps, like clever children, we should learn to watch our betters, trusting that when they laugh something is funny. For how can one be expected to feel a wind which only blows far above his head? Well, look up! Watch the giant sequoias. When those great boughs quake, something is stirring.

Saint Luke, in his Gospel, records the following remarkable statement: "In that same hour [Jesus] rejoiced in the Holy Spirit and said, 'I thank thee Father, Lord of heaven and earth, that thou hast hidden these things from the wise and understanding and revealed them to babes. . . . ' " Might not that have rung the kingdom with laughter? Indeed, we do feel a little uncomfortable with the euphoria Jesus felt at the very thought! Our eyes may even dart a bit.

Your good friend,
Robert

Dear Dad,

Laura still. You must be very weary of this. I can almost feel your eyes running across these words in disappointment. I don't blame you. I'm sick to death of the subject. Who would have ever guessed the aftermath to be longer than the thing itself. But even now these words seem dishonest. I write as if I clearly know it's over. It isn't. Embarrassing, humiliating, alarming, exhausting as it all is, I must admit that the part of me which still hangs on is the greater part.

Laura is completely unambivalent in her goals. I hadn't reckoned on that. She knows exactly what she wants and exactly what she'll do to get it. What a disadvantage it is to have two voices in me when she has only one in her. She has asked me to move in with her. We will keep it as "platonic" as I wish, she promises. There are two bedrooms in the apartment.

There it is. You don't know how hard it was to write that paragraph, to put it down in bald prose and to have you know that the proposition was not dismissed out of hand; to have you know that, even now, the thing is playing through my mind, that desperate rationalizations are being tried and retried almost at this very minute. I don't want anyone to know this is happening, least of all you. But since I see now how startlingly easy hypocrisy is (surely no one ever decided to become a hypocrite on principle), I make myself write this down. And I hope I shall get it into the mailbox. I foresee an amusing scene when I change my mind the moment after the letter has slipped from my hand. If I call from jail don't be alarmed. I will only have been arrested for trying to crack open a U.S. Postal Service box.

Will you think it all a joke if I enclose "Passion on a Short Leash"?

Jeff

Passion on a Short Leash

I'll tell you what it's like when she walks through the room.
   Did you ever reach to pet the cat and have it shrink
   demure
   conforming to your curved palm
   like a casting to a mold
   but wouldn't let you touch a hair
   of it? Stayed just a quarter inch away
   from every last fur-thirsty nerve
   of your frustrated hand—advancing now to your retreat
   retreating now to your advance—until
   you lurch out of your deep-set chair
   sending lap books everywhere
   and grab and miss and sprawling
   even miss the corner-disappearing tail. Oh!
Well.
It's like that.
   Or did you ever save the best bite
   miserlike and save it slightly to the side
   neat-cut and ready with the taste
   you want to finish with, want to leave the table with?
   And then
   with one drink left to rinse it down
   you blunder-fork it, hapless see it slip
   between the plate and waiting lip
   and then the dog gets to it first almost before the floor
   leaving you, splay-fingered ne'er-do-well
   to quell
   the taste-bud riot screaming
   for your blood, the fork's, the floor's, the dog's.
Like that.

Paul,

Well, yes, it is what the spider said to the fly. But even if the con man says "trust me" or "try it, you'll like it" for ulterior reasons, friends and lovers often say the exact same words in complete good faith. Bear in mind, too, that when you're invited through a door you are not given a choice between making a decision and not making a decision. You will decide.

As to whether the door is a way into something or a way out of something, it depends on the point of view. (Going into a house may be expressed as getting out of the weather.) Suppose you were already in the web and that door was the way to freedom. Then where would your spider be and what would he be saying?

You are invited to stand fast by some voices and to go through the door by others. And we say, get to know your spiders. Even if you've not been devoured, you may be very snugly caught. Examine a spider's web sometime. It's often loaded with uneaten victims. He'll get around to them. Before you barricade the door, be very sure which side the enemy is on.

We're greatly relieved about Edith, needless to say. For the first time since the crisis began Maggie has mentally unpacked her bags, I think. Still in the event of any further need please give us a chance to help out.

I didn't know Bruce Stidham well, but I remember how close you two were. What a distress it must be for you to see him go down and not be able to help.

With love,
Robert

Dear Jeff,

Well, I've gotten no call from jail! And the letter was mailed. Congratulations. No joke.

"Passion on a Short Leash" is effective for me. I take it as I think it came—a pressure relief valve. Some would say it was therapy for you, the muse as nurse, but we have better medicine than that.

I'm not as disappointed as you imagine. Rather, I'm reminded of what that struggle is like. Let's see if you are like me: I am embarrassed to be tempted sexually, embarrassed that the temptation is so low, so . . . well, salacious, so easily imagined and recreated in the bystander's mind. How humiliating for someone to know that at a particular point in time some particular stimulus sets me panting.

I think the embarrassment is easily misunderstood, though. It is not precisely an embarrassment at sin. For much the same phenomena may occur in the innocent context of conjugal union. One may be set panting there, too. No. I think it is humiliation to know that the high and mighty in us, the proud cerebral fortress (which we fancy our true headquarters) is so easily taken by this vulgar fellow of the streets, the body. But we are warned most solemnly in Scripture that the body is no more dangerous than the mind. In fact, Jesus was rather gentler with harlots than with hypocrites (albeit, countenancing neither's sin).

Here, most clearly, is seen the havoc of rebellion. The mind and the body conspire to rebel against God. The mind, being the aristocrat, assumes that after the revolution the low, servile body will, of course, recognize the "natural" rule of the mind. But rebellion breeds rebellion, and the body makes its own revolution. It is bloody civil war: the ragged hordes of Appetite swarming against the disciplined ranks of Pride. Depending on the fortunes of war, we may end up with a lecher, a drunk, a glutton or, if the other side dominates, an ascetic, a snob or a prig. It is these latter who pretend no civil war is going on. Their entire affaire d'etat is the production of the propaganda that all within its borders is calm and in order. Hypocrisy becomes an occupation.

Only the healing of the original rebellion can stop the fighting. Repentance must be directed toward that end. So I think it's sometimes necessary to throw off that superficial embarrassment, the embarrassment of animality, of having physical drives, in order to get at the rebellion against God's rule. For it is that prior rebellion that enfranchises the secondary revolt of the appetites.

Isn't it remarkable how God keeps us supplied with endless particular material on which to learn obedience! Jesus, himself, remember, is said to have learned obedience by the things (plural particulars) which he suffered. So the Christian life turns out to be a series of obstacles. We imagine that if we could just get through this present difficulty we could get on with the business of living the Christian life. But the obstacles turn out to be the very tissue of which that life is made. When we somehow get through this one, this present erotic distraction, this present financial crisis, this present illness, lo, here is something else to face. We wish to be through with this tedious business of multiplication tables in order to get on with mathematics. Then we turn the page and find a chapter titled, "Division."

The experience is so universal among Christians that I think we may almost identify a rule here. This present difficulty, this backwater we're caught in (while everyone else, of course, is sailing clear upon the real current) *is* the mainstream. So we paddle on, slough after slough, able to mark our progress only by thinking back: yes, a few hours ago we were in reeds and now we're out. But what's this brackish mess up ahead? Will we never get back on the river!

With love and appreciation,
Dad

P.S. I'm sticking in "The Pharisee's Consolation" as my own confession. I must not deny (after your candor) that there's autobiography in it.

The Pharisee's Consolation

One wouldn't ever do the thing, of course.
Wouldn't ever do it.
Mustn't.
But . . . oh, to think about it, though.
To run one's mind along it like a tongue
moves over a dissolving sweet.
Sucking on it,
slipping it back in the secret cheek
to taste its slow-releasing liquor for an afternoon.
It is enough, almost.

Dear Robert,

But why keep us awake only to weep? Oh, I have
hewn me a tolerable enough cave. It's short on light
but at least dry and snug from the winds. Don't I
know the grim statistics, though? What of that roiling
mob out there in the wild weather? Is such a riot of
misery beside the point to him? Incidental is it to the
Grand Scheme? The mewlings of cats beneath the
throne, is it? Why is tragedy, slow and undramatic,
nearly the whole program? Or if this is but the over-
ture, then what is to be dreaded at the curtain's rising?

Bruce Stidham is dead. We just heard this morning.
Sleeping pills.

And Edith is nearly as exasperating as you. Oh,
she makes no claim to insider's knowledge. She
simply ignores the ghastly cleavage altogether. The
God of her hymns and prayers need never explain to
her why love and joy is burned into our brains as that
which ought to be—and then left there, in our brains,
to taunt us against the presence of almost all we see.

Give me your line on this again. I can't seem to
keep it clear. I must sound very cynical today. In fact,
I am weary with this awful subject. But you I love
and would know better the ground between us. How
far must we go to meet again?

Paul

Dear Paul,

The news of Bruce's death hits very hard. I know what a heartbreak it must be for you. And I do understand your questions. But I think I am probably the least likely Christian in the whole world to be of any help to you. (Does "help" offend you here?) You see, I have too many parts affection per parts love. I am not able to be as hard on you as I think you require. Love would see the problem and cut at it immediately. I would mince and spare.

There are two kingdoms. The cleavage you speak of is horribly there between the two and horribly wide. The hope of love and joy burned in your brain (or somewhere deeper) is but the flag of the other kingdom planted here in this. You need no vivid description of this kingdom we are in, none of us do. But it may help to be told that an evil prince has come to power here (by permission, yes, but that is too deep a story for me to explain) and that the very word *gospel* means "good news" about a rescue party from that other kingdom which has already landed and is this moment taking on emigrants.

Yours,
Robert

Dear Dad,

Laura came again, for the last time I think. She was strangely cool and clear headed.

The pictures we are given of our proper relation to God, bought with a price, not our own, slaves bound to duty, are helpful and instructive and indicate the frame of mind within which one must attempt to stay. But under the strain of some sharp desire to please one's self, the pictures, the parables, the rich analogies sometimes fall away, leaving the issue reduced to obedience only—clear and unadorned choice, the cold, hard edge of a blade which cuts and divides, leaving us to fall either on our own side or his.

She left somewhat melodramatically, posturing as the spurned woman and making elaborate promises which, I think, this time, she'll be able to keep.

Coincidentally (and mercifully) the same day I had the first interesting conversation with another girl S.L. (since Laura). She's quiet and confident and, I suspect, deep. We shall see. Her name is Charlotte and she insists on Char, a frivolous insistence which seems not to fit with the rest of her. But one can't have everything. Need I add, she is a Christian. I have become very scrupulous about such qualifications.

Love,
Jeff

My God, Bobby! Paul dead? My flight arrives 10:25 Wednesday morning. Tell Edith I'm thinking of her constantly. Earlier this evening I sat paralyzed for an hour over a white sheet of paper headed "My dearest Edith." The words I finally wrote were sheer desolation. There must be some consolation in all this, Bobby, but I can't discover it tonight. I must see you and we must talk.

Philip

Dear Jeff,

Your support during this past week has been the gift of God to your mother and me. The reminder of priorities which always accompanies death and funerals made our 2:00 A.M. conversations so full of realities.

Edith is still here and we're trying to get her to stay on for Christmas. She sees the return to the empty house as something that needs to be faced sooner than later, but I think she will stay. She's remarkably sturdy about everything. How I admire her.

She talks a great deal and we mostly listen. She said the doctor told her Paul suffered a massive blood clot in his heart and that apparently nothing could have been done to predict or prevent it. It is strange that the inevitability of it should give us a little flicker of comfort, but somehow it does.

We can hardly wait for your Christmas visit, and are in total agreement about your bringing Char. Please do! She sounds like a delight. Your mother and Edith are already at work redoing the downstairs guest room. I hear mumbling about wallpaper patterns and perhaps a new carpet. It's a great tonic just now.

God keep you,
Dad

Bobby,

I hardly know which is stranger, Paul's death or all the astonishing things you said to me when I was there. But none of it is as strange as the sense of being followed, hunted almost, by Someone ever since we talked. I am appalled that so close after a crushing tragedy I find a spring in my step and a tune in me somewhere trying to get itself hummed. Such an immoderate roller coaster ride has very nearly done me in. I sit exhausted before a crackling fire and barely manage the energy to write these words. But with the exhaustion there is a delicious quietness in which I find myself startlingly close to saying yes to Him.

I've decided to accept your invitation for the Christmas holidays and have already begun to compile a list of the questions which seem to be spurting up in me now at the rate of one or two an hour.

Your friend,
Philip